THE BOY AT THE DIKE

A DUTCH FOLKTALE

Retold by M. J. York •Illustrated by Laura Freeman

The Child's World®
1980 Lookout Drive • Mankato, MN 56003-1705
800-599-READ • www.childsworld.com

Acknowledgments
The Child's World®: Mary Berendes, Publishing Director
The Design Lab: Kathleen Petelinsek, Design
Red Line Editorial: Editorial direction

ISBN 9781614732198
LCCN 2012932435

Printed in the United States of America
Mankato, MN
July 2012
PA02123

any years ago, before your parents or your grandparents were born, a little boy named Peter lived near the sea. In Peter's country, Holland, unlike in many countries, the sea is higher than the land. The people of Holland built high, strong walls to keep the water out. We call these walls dikes.

Peter and every other little child in Holland knew how important the dikes were. If the sea came through the dikes, it could drown all the farms and villages in Holland. Every little child in Holland learned to watch for water coming through the dikes, even the smallest trickle. Even a small hole, no bigger than the smallest child's finger, needed to be stopped.

Early one day, Peter's mother handed Peter a sack of fresh cookies. She told him, "Take these cookies to your friend the blind man. Follow the dike so you don't get lost, and be sure to be home before supper!"

"Of course, Mother," replied Peter. "I am seven years old now. I am almost grown up! I will visit my friend and be home before supper."

Happily, Peter set off along the dike toward his friend's home. He skipped through the fields and meadows. He startled a rabbit and watched it leap away. He felt the warm sunshine and smelled the bright flowers. He looked out to sea and saw ships sailing far away.

Even though the sun was shining, Peter noticed that the water was high and the waves were tall. "I know why my father calls the water 'angry,'" he thought. "The sea looks as though it is trying to get in through the dike!"

At last, Peter reached the home of his
friend the blind man. He gave his friend
the fresh cookies. Then he told the blind
man about his walk along the dike, the
rabbit, the sunshine, the flowers, and
the ships. He stayed until the afternoon,
sharing stories with his friend.

At last, the clock struck three o'clock. Peter realized he had better leave, or he would be late for supper. So he set off from his friend's house.

He followed the dike toward home. He was walking quickly so he would not be late for supper. Peter watched the sun over his shoulder. It was sinking closer and closer to the sea.

Peter was almost running along the dike when he heard a tiny trickling noise. He stopped and looked closely at the dike. There! He saw a small hole in the dike. Water was coming through and trickling down the dike.

Peter knew he did not have time to run home and warn someone. The water could burst through the dike at any time. He knew he had to stop the water himself. Quickly, he stuck his small finger in the hole. The water stopped!

Peter felt brave and strong. "I can keep back all the angry waters of the sea with my little finger!" he thought. But Peter was stuck. If he moved, the water would come through again. The sun set, and Peter was still stuck beside the dike.

He yelled loudly for someone to help him. But no one heard him and no one came by.

At Peter's home, his mother was growing worried. Supper had come and gone, and still Peter was not home. She thought, "Peter must have stayed overnight with his friend the blind man. I will have to scold him when he returns." But yet she worried.

Hours passed. Peter was cold and a
little scared in the dark. His legs and his
arms were cramped. He was very tired,
but he had to stay awake. He had to keep
his finger in the dike.

The night passed slowly for Peter at the dike and his mother at home. Neither slept all night. Finally, morning came. Peter stretched his legs and his free arm, but he kept his finger in the dike. He was getting hungry, but still no one came.

At last, Peter heard someone coming. It was a farmer, going to work in his field. "Help me!" Peter called softly, his voice quiet and tired. Fortunately, the man heard him and came running.

Peter told his story, and the farmer went for help. Quickly, the farmer returned with other men. They stopped the hole in the dike. Finally, Peter was free.

The farmer said, "Thank you, Peter. You are a brave boy, and you kept the angry water from flooding my field." And the farmer carried Peter home. And now the children of Holland learn the story of brave Peter, the little boy who kept back the angry waters of the sea.

Holland

FOLKTALES

The Boy at the Dike takes place in Holland, in the western part of the Netherlands, on the North Sea. Can you picture where Holland is on a map of the world? It is north of Paris, France, and east of London, England.

People who live in Holland speak the Dutch language, and are called Dutch people. Since they live so close to the ocean, they have to manage all the water they live around, including the sea and the rivers that flow into it. Dikes help them hold the waters back so their towns do not flood. Read the story again and you'll notice the words "angry waters." Can you imagine what angry waters look like? What do you think happy, or calm, waters look like?

The Boy at the Dike is a folktale, or a popular story that has been told so many times that its first author is unknown. The folktale is now like a legend, or a very well-known tale that people know by heart and learn lessons from.

The story's "little hero," Peter, is very admirable, someone that we can look up to. He is observant, seeing the smallest of holes that others probably didn't notice. He is courageous, lasting an entire, cold night plugging the hole to save his town. *The Boy at the Dike* shows us the power of one person's bravery. Seemingly small acts can make a big difference—even save a village! What small acts of kindness or bravery have you done or seen?

ABOUT THE ILLUSTRATOR

Laura Freeman has been drawing pictures for as long as she can remember, and illustrating books since 1998. She's from New York City, but currently lives in Atlanta with her husband, their two children, and two cats.